PUFFIN BOOKS

## Shark Sunday

Mary Rayner is the best-selling author and illustrator of the *Garth Pig* picture books. She has three children and lives in Wiltshire.

# MARY RAYNER
# Shark Sunday

PUFFIN BOOKS

PUFFIN BOOKS

Published by the Penguin Group
Penguin Books Ltd, 27 Wrights Lane, London W8 5TZ, England
Penguin Putnam Inc., 375 Hudson Street, New York,
New York 10014, USA
Penguin Books Australia Ltd, Ringwood, Victoria, Australia
Penguin Books Canada Ltd, 10 Alcorn Avenue, Toronto,
Ontario, Canada M4V 3B2
Penguin Books (NZ) Ltd, Cnr Rosedale and Airborne Roads, Albany,
Auckland, New Zealand

Penguin Books Ltd, Registered Offices: Harmondsworth,
Middlesex, England

First published by Viking 1997
Published in Puffin Books 1998
1 3 5 7 9 10 8 6 4 2

Set in Palatino

Made and printed in England by Clays Ltd, St Ives plc

British Library Cataloguing in Publication Data
A CIP catalogue record for this book is available from
the British Library

ISBN 0–140–38185–6

*For Louise, Robbie, Nicola,*
*and Jamie*

# One

Gordon was fed up. He hated car boot sales. Why did his mum always want to go to them? She'd insisted on stopping off on the way home from his Saturday morning's football, and now she was taking ages looking at a whole lot of china spread out on a table.

If she was much longer he wouldn't have time to do all that long subtraction that Miss Knight had set him. It wasn't fair. No one else had got homework. They weren't supposed to *have* homework.

Just because he'd got the last lot all wrong. He'd been fine before he moved

up into Miss Knight's class. He kicked a
stone crossly. *And* it had all got to be
done for Monday. He hated Miss
Knight. Horrid Miss Knight.

"Buy a nice bunch of heather, my
darling?" said a plump woman, barring
his way. She had pink made-up cheeks
and dark hair curling out from under a
scarf, and was holding out a bunch of
purple flowers.

Gordon scowled at her. "I haven't got any money."

"Well," she said amiably. "Shake my hand then, and I'll wish you luck."

Gordon could see his mother leaning further across the table to unstack another pile of plates. There was no escape yet.

Reluctantly he put out a hand to the woman in the scarf, and she squeezed it. He snatched it back and wandered over to a big battered old car which was parked alongside. There was so much mud on the back windscreen that the wiper had made a fan-shaped window through it. Piled round the back on the ground were cardboard boxes full of household junk.

Gordon pulled one of the boxes towards him to see what was in it. There was an old electric kettle without any

flex, two battered lamp-shades, a red
thermos flask, a bundle of old knives
tied together with string, a small
blackened oil-lamp, and a pair of old
walking boots stiff with age.

Gordon lifted out the boots. They
were much too big. Then he saw that
underneath them was a football, real
leather, a bit flat but it might pump

up OK.

The woman in the scarf was watching him. "Yours for fifty pence the lot," she said.

"Wait," said Gordon. He ran over to his mother. She was turning over a blue and white bowl in her hands, and smiling happily. "Look," she whispered to him. "What a bargain!"

This was his chance. He asked for the fifty pence and she handed it over without a murmur.

Gordon loaded his box of purchases on to the back seat of their car and his mother bundled up her mac and wedged her bowl safely beside it. Gordon sang "Ten Green Bottles" all the way home to Selkirk Road, and they had baked beans for lunch.

After lunch Gordon took his cardboard box up to his room to see

what could be done with the football.
He needed a pump.

He ran down to the alley at the side of
the house to see if there was a bicycle-
pump anywhere in the lean-to shed, but
although he searched high and low he
couldn't find one. Rats, thought
Gordon, plodding back upstairs.

He took out the rest of the junk. The
knives might just come in handy. He

undid the string and laid them out in a row. They were old, with yellow bone handles and rounded blades, rusted here and there. Perhaps he could swap them at school if he sharpened them first?

He fetched a sock to try to get the rust off, but although he made a right mess of the sock they still looked just as bad. He lifted out the little lamp and wiped some of the grime off it.

There was a faint twangling sound coming from somewhere. He must have left his radio on. Gordon checked, but no, it was switched off. The twangling noise grew louder. Then he noticed a wisp of greenish smoke floating above the pillow on his bed, and he could hear – very faint – some foreign-sounding singing.

The smoke thickened and swirled

around. It was making his throat tingle and his eyes smart. Gordon backed towards the window, but before he could open it the smoke began to swirl round faster and faster, until it made a spinning column just above his bed.

The twangling instrument and the singing stopped, and there was a burst of deep laughter, a man's laughter.

The smoke cleared, and there, sitting on his bed, was a stranger in a turban. He had dark curving moustaches, under which he was grinning at Gordon from ear to ear. His legs were crossed at the ankles and he was wearing loose white pantaloons. He uncrossed his ankles, stretched out his legs and twisted his bare feet outwards in two circles. The soles were hard and crinkled like old leather.

"I thank you," he said. "I have waited

many years for this. What is your will,
O Master? Your wish is my command."

Oh wow, thought Gordon, the genie of
the lamp!

# Two

Gordon looked down at the lamp,
which he was still holding. Where he
had rubbed it with his sock there was a
small cleaner shiny patch.

"Yes, you are right," said the stranger,
reading Gordon's mind. "I am a djinn, a
djinni, a genie, and you have three
wishes. I have great magical powers."

Gordon stared at him for several
moments. "I'll have to think," he said,
completely taken aback by the
suddenness of it all.

"Anything at all I can do," said the
djinn. "You have but to order me.
Would you care for a hundred camels

perhaps?" He extended a golden arm
and drew a wavy line in the air, so that
Gordon could at once imagine a long
line of camels padding across tawny
dunes of sand.

"Um, no-o," said Gordon, frowning.

The djinn's face fell. For a moment he surveyed the ceiling, then he half closed his eyes and looked dreamy. "I could conjure for you a harem of eighty maidens, with faces like moons and eyes like dark pools, each one more beautiful than the last – "

"Hey," said Gordon, who could feel his face growing pink. "Don't be daft. I'm not grown up yet."

The djinn opened his eyes and wriggled on the bed. "I am sorry, Master, I was getting carried away. It has been a long time since I took on human shape. I was not thinking how old you are. No, that would not be a correct wish for you."

He considered for a while, then held out both arms and drew a huge dome in the air. "How would you like a palace of white marble inlaid with precious stones, with paved courtyards and fountains sparkling in the shadows, and as many slaves as you desire?"

Gordon thought about a palace like that squashed in behind the bike-shed next to 25 Selkirk Road and began to giggle helplessly. Then he became serious. "Don't rush me. These are all the kind of things that you might want. They aren't right for me."

The djinn shrugged. "I was only trying. Well, at least I have made you laugh."

Gordon sat down on the carpet at the djinn's feet and thought. What would be a good wish to ask for? Win the lottery? No, he wouldn't be allowed to, he was too young. Be King? Not much fun, when you thought about it. There must be *something*. What had he been doing

before the djinn appeared?

He glanced up uncertainly. "What I'd really like is to have that football as good as new again. That's if you know about football."

"I have great magical power," said the djinn with dignity. "As I told you. And besides, football is not unknown in Arabia these days, I keep meaning to learn the rules. Is it your considered

wish? Your first wish? If I do this you
will only have two wishes left. You may
recall me at any time by rubbing the
lamp."

Gordon nodded, and held out the
sagging football. Asking for stupendous
riches could wait till next time.

The djinn passed his hands twice over
the ball, muttered a few words in a

foreign language, and then with another
deep chuckle he was gone, leaving only

a faint wisp of green smoke which floated lazily up to the ceiling and then vanished.

Gordon looked down. The football gleamed taut and new in his hands. "Oh, excellent!" he shouted, and ran downstairs and out into the back garden to try it out.

# Three

Gordon got up early on Monday morning. He'd managed to struggle through the maths for Miss Knight last thing before he'd gone to bed, and now he planned to go to school in plenty of time so they could all play with his new football. Good old djinn.

He was careful not to forget the piece of paper with his work on it, and put it into his school-bag with his lunch-box. Just before he left a thought struck him. He ran back up to his room and rubbed a finger around the base of the little lamp.

He held his breath. Sure enough, there

was a loud downward twanging chord, and then green wisps of smoke appeared. They drifted into a swirling column, gathered speed, spun round and round and then dissolved into the figure of the djinn. He was standing in the middle of the carpet with his arms crossed, looking down at Gordon.

"What is your will, O Master?"

"I haven't got a wish," said Gordon. "I just thought you might like to come along to school and see us playing football – learn the rules. You'd have to make yourself invisible, of course."

"That is most thoughtful," said the djinn. "I would enjoy that. Off you go, and I shall be there."

Gordon hurried downstairs again, picked up his football and ran out of the front door.

They played a terrific game. The time flew by, and Gordon was only just

aware of all the rest of the school's
pupils crossing the playground to go
into school as he tackled and dodged.
Somewhere the bell was ringing, but
Gordon had his eye on the ball. He
kicked it, neatly curling it just inside the
post to score, then ran to pick it up. He
was just panting in through the hall to

the cloakroom when he met Miss Knight.

"Ah," she said. "Gordon. Late again, I see. I'll have that ball if you don't mind. A little more concentration on maths and a little less on football would not hurt, young man. And I am waiting for the work I set you to be handed in."

Gordon could not believe it. He held on to the football, tight, and glared at her, standing his ground.

"Come on," she said, holding out both her hands. "Give it here."

Just then the Headmaster came out of his room. "Do as Miss Knight tells you," he said to Gordon, and swept on down the corridor. Reluctantly Gordon held out the football and Miss Knight tucked it under one arm and went into the staff-room.

Gordon stomped into the cloakroom

close to tears. He rummaged in his
school-bag for the page of sums. I hate
her, he thought. There was nobody in
the cloakroom. He stamped on the floor
in fury and shouted out loud, "I wish
Miss Knight would take a very long
walk along a short plank over an ocean
full of sharks!"

A wisp of green smoke floated past the wash-basins and hovered over Gordon's peg. There was a deep chuckle, and a voice said, "I hear, O Master, and I obey . . ." The voice faded out of the window, leaving Gordon standing with his mouth open.

Silly old djinn, thought Gordon, he doesn't know there aren't any sharks in a school playground, and he smiled to himself. He picked up the piece of paper and walked into the classroom.

# Four

Miss Knight was clearly surprised that he had done the work. Later, when she handed it back, he saw that he'd actually got all the answers right, and that she'd put "Well done" in red at the bottom. At the end of the afternoon she told him to come to the staff-room, and gave him back his football.

He was sauntering back along the road home swinging his school-bag when there was a sudden puff of green smoke and the djinn fell into step beside him. Gordon looked round wildly to see if anyone else had seen him.

"I am only visible to you," said the

djinn. "So how was my subtraction? Were you not pleased?"

"*Your* subtraction?" said Gordon, startled.

"Yes. I corrected all your answers before you handed it in. Did you not know that the numerals that you use come from Arabic? And that algebra came to you from Arabia?"

"I certainly didn't," said Gordon. "And we don't do algebra yet." He was not sure whether to be pleased or cross.

"What *do* they teach you?" said the djinn with a sigh.

"But I didn't ask you to," said Gordon, worried. "Has that taken one of my wishes?"

The djinn laughed and patted his arm. "No, no, I was amusing myself while you were all playing the football, that is all. I was standing beside your school-bag. I have to keep practising my powers, or they would lose their strength. You are not angry with me? It was good, it made her give you back your ball."

Gordon thought. Then he said, "Sugar! I thought I'd understood that maths. Now I'm not sure."

"No problem," said the djinn, waving an arm airily. "If you will stand still a

moment. And this time, O Master, listen carefully."

Gordon stopped dead in his tracks. He found himself thinking back to Thursday afternoon. He was in the classroom, and Miss Knight was writing on the board. This time he didn't look out of the window or think about Saturday's match, he was looking at what she'd written, and hearing her voice explaining it. Then she wrote up

another subtraction sum. And he could
understand how it was done.

Oh wow, he thought, brilliant! Now I
really understand. What a useful spirit
to have around!

Aloud he said, "Thanks, thanks a lot,"
but the djinn had vanished.

"You see," said a deep voice. "You can
do it for yourself when you try."

In the air where he had been standing
was a subtraction sum written in green

smoke. The smoke drifted down the street ahead of Gordon and then re-formed into the answer. Gordon laughed out loud and swung in at his gate.

The rest of the week went well. The djinn did not reappear, but Gordon played a great deal of football. Miss

Knight was pleased with his work, and
he even began to enjoy school.

On the Wednesday night his mother
let him set his alarm so that he could
listen to the cricket on the radio in bed.
England were playing a one-day
international against Australia. Soon the
Test series for the Ashes would begin.

On the Friday afternoon Miss Knight had them all studying a map of the world.

"I know one or two of you've been listening to the cricket," she said. "Now I want you to find the cities in Australia where they'll be playing the Tests."

They found Perth, Sydney and Melbourne. Then Miss Knight held up a torch and spun the globe round to show how when the sun was shining on one half it was day, while the other half was in shadow and it was night.

"That's why you've had to listen to the cricket in the middle of the night," she said, showing them how it would be daytime in Australia. "They're ahead of us," she said, "and America is behind. I have relatives – an uncle and an aunt – who live north of Brisbane." And she pointed out the spot.

This was a novel way of learning geography, thought Gordon happily. At this rate Miss Knight would soon be learning the rules of football and pointing out Wembley. Good old Miss Knight. And then she said something that made his blood run cold.

"I'm going to spend three weeks with them over the holidays. Imagine, while you're all shivering away here with frost and snow and Christmas and dark nights and short days, I shall be lying in the sun and having barbecues on the beach!"

Oh no, thought Gordon. Not barbecues on the beach. What about my wish in the cloakroom? Oh, djinn, what have you done?

Miss Knight went on, "I'm actually going this weekend, because that was the only flight with a seat left – it gets very booked up at Christmas. Which means," and she smiled round at the entire class, "that I shall miss the last two days of term. The Headmaster has kindly let me go early. I want you all to be very good, because you remember Miss Cavendish who came in when I

45

had flu? She'll be coming in to look after
you. So I'll say goodbye and happy
Christmas now."

The minute the bell went for the end
of school, Gordon hurried to get his

things. No one could understand why he didn't wait and play in the playground as usual, but he muttered "Got to go," and raced home.

He threw down his school-bag and charged up to his room.

Frantically he rubbed the base of the lamp.

After what seemed like an endless wait a little curl of green smoke appeared and began slowly to thicken.

Come on, come on, said Gordon, his teeth clenched.

The smoke circled round lazily and then picked up a little speed. Gradually it grew into the shape of the smiling djinn.

"This is not a joke," said Gordon, scowling at him.

The djinn stopped smiling. "What is your will, O Master?"

"It's about what I said on Monday in the school cloakroom," said Gordon.

"Ah, you mean your second wish. I've enjoyed that one. I have done well, have I not? Your Miss Knight flies out by Qantas tomorrow, and within forty-eight hours from now she will be on an Australian beach. It was quite difficult to arrange, but I managed. I had to dredge up some long-lost relations for her."

Gordon stared at him. He was quite serious. "But I don't want her eaten by sharks now," he wailed. "She's been quite nice to me."

The djinn sat down on Gordon's bed and put his head in his hands. "Master, you do not understand. My magic is exceedingly powerful, as I thought I told you. What I have done I cannot

undo. You made the wish. It must now run its course."

"Oh sugar," said Gordon, biting his thumb. "Whatever are we going to do?"

The djinn said in a tired voice, "It is not *we*. The decisions – the orders –

have to come from you. I am but your slave. If I have now displeased you I am sorry for it, but I cannot prevent Miss Knight going to Australia. That will now happen, you cannot unwish it. I shall go now, if you have no further need of me. Farewell, O Master." And with these words he vanished.

# Five

Gordon did not sleep well that night.
Over and over again he tried to recall
exactly what he'd said in the cloakroom,
but it was no good, he couldn't.

He woke early, and tossed and turned
in the dark. Finally he pulled himself
up to a sitting position and switched on
the bedside light. It was only six
o'clock.

"Oh," he groaned out loud.
"Whatever was it I said?"

He stared at the blank wall opposite
the bed, fighting to remember, and
suddenly a little wriggle of green
smoke appeared in front of it. It was

moving along! It was writing. Gordon
read the words with difficulty as they
danced up and down.

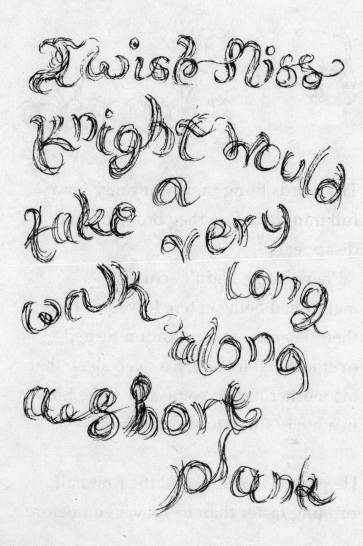

I wish Miss Knight would take a very long walk along a short plank

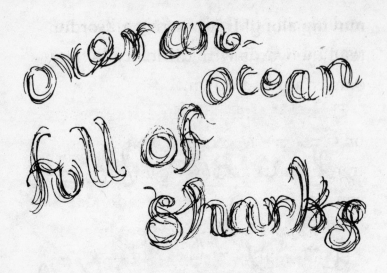

over an ocean full of sharks

The words hung there unevenly for a full minute before they broke up and disappeared.

Phew! So he hadn't actually mentioned being eaten. It was all right then. Thanks, genie. Gordon turned over and fell into such a deep sleep that his mother had to come and wake him in a hurry for Saturday football.

He played brilliantly all the first half, running faster than he'd ever run before and placing the ball exactly where he wanted it to go. They were leading two nil.

Then just after half-time, the keeper on Gordon's team was given the most tremendous crack on the jaw by somebody jumping for a header. He had to go off and Gordon was put in goal.

Standing there, trying to keep warm, Gordon felt a sneaky bit of worry come back and begin to nag. Supposing it wasn't all right for Miss Knight, supposing even though he hadn't actually *said* so, something terrible happened to her? Then it would all be his fault.

What was it the djinn had said? *"The decisions — the orders — are yours."*

Nobody would ever know, he told himself. But it was no good. *I* would know, he thought.

Just then the ball whammed out of nowhere past his right shoulder and zinged into the back of the net.

"Oh, *Gor*don," shouted his team-mates. "That should've been an easy save!"

From then on it was disaster all the way. Whether it was because he'd never

been much good in goal, or because of
lack of sleep, or because of the worry,
whatever it was, Gordon let in three
more goals.

"What's up?" said his mother when
she came to pick him up. "You look a bit
miserable."

"We lost, and it was all my fault." No
way could he tell her the main trouble.

"Well, never mind, cheer up," she
said. "I'm taking you Christmas
shopping this afternoon – that'll take
your mind off it."

She was right, it did, for the time
being, and for the rest of the day
everything was fine. When he went to
bed he lay there thinking about what to
say he wanted for Christmas, and
dropped off to sleep without having
decided.

After some while he woke up with a

start. It was dark. First he remembered about the Christmas presents. He switched on the light, got out of bed and padded over to his school-bag to fetch some paper for a list. Then it all came back to him.

He could not stop wondering what to do. He decided to call up the genie again.

When he appeared, Gordon said, "Now, this is just a question. Don't go and act on it yet. But for my third wish, can't I just wish Miss Knight saved?"

The djinn sucked in his breath and looked unhappy. "But that is surely an unwinding of your second wish, which I am not empowered to do. We could try, but I could not be certain that it would work."

"So you mean I might *waste* my last wish?"

The djinn nodded gloomily.

"How far has she got?" asked Gordon.

The djinn cheered up. "You would like
to watch that wish in progress? No
problem. That is well within my
powers. Sit on your bed and keep your
eyes on the blank wall there."

He muttered a couple of commands in a foreign language and came to sit on the bed beside Gordon. A cloud of green smoke formed in front of the wall, and then dissolved into a distant view of a Qantas aeroplane, flying against a blue sky through banked cloud.

Then the picture changed to the inside of the jumbo jet.

It had *two* aisles, Gordon noticed, and an air stewardess was pushing a trolley towards them. And yes, there was plump Miss Knight, leaning across and asking for duty-free perfume. Miss Knight, buying perfume! Goodness, whatever next!

The picture changed back to the long shot. They watched as the plane flew on.

"Enough?" asked the djinn.

"Yes, thanks," said Gordon. There was still plenty of time to think of something. The 747 faded from the wall, and the banked clouds turned from white to green and thinned into small shreds which floated up to the ceiling and then vanished.

When Gordon swung round the djinn too had gone. He put out the light and fell asleep again.

# Six

When Gordon next woke, it was to the sound of church bells down the road.

It was daylight.

"I do not like that noise," grumbled a familiar deep voice. "Our call to prayer, now, is much more melodious." The djinn was sitting cross-legged on the far side of the room with his hands over his ears. "Yours goes back and back over the same notes."

"Well, tough," said Gordon. "I can't stop the bells." What time was it? Where had the jumbo got to?

The djinn read his thoughts. "It landed

a couple of hours ago. Soon your Miss
Knight will be going to the beach with
her uncle and aunt."

Gordon suddenly knew that he
couldn't just lie in bed and wait to see
what happened. Australia was ten

hours behind, wasn't it? He glanced at his clock and started to do the subtraction in his head. Ten hours back from now. That made it before midnight, still night-time.

"Djinn," he said. "We've plenty of time. You will have to get me there before she walks that plank."

"O Master," wailed the djinn. "No, you are wrong. You are taking away ten hours. You must add. Australia – Queensland, where she is – is ten hours *ahead*. Do you not remember, she told you, showed you with the globe? Even now they are packing up the supper barbecue things before going down to the beach."

Gordon leaped out of bed and hurled his sweater over his head. "Summon up every magical power you've got then! How soon can you fly there?"

"The jumbo takes around twenty-two hours, but for me it will be nearer twenty-two minutes."

"Right," said Gordon through clenched teeth, tying up his trainers. "Then this is my third wish. Forget anything about palaces or riches. Just

get me there in time."

"I hear, O Master, and I obey. Stand
behind me on the chair and put your
hands around my neck, and whatever
you do, do not let go."

Gordon scrambled on to the chair and
clasped the djinn's thick neck. There

was a roar like thunder, and a blinding
flash. Gordon closed his eyes as a
mighty wind hit his face and arms and
shoulders.

When he opened them again he could
see the church and Selkirk Road
dwindling in the distance below as they
climbed into the clouds. The horizon
tilted down sharply as they banked,
turned and shot off towards the newly
risen sun.

The cloud blanket below was moving like speeded-up film. Gordon turned his head, and saw that the djinn had spread out enormous golden feathered wings.

They overtook a couple of planes crossing the Alps. So fast were they going that the full-sized planes seemed to be scarcely moving at all, just hanging in the air. Gordon waved with one arm to the passengers looking out of the windows, but no one waved back.

We must be just a blur to them, he thought. Or invisible.

It was hard work holding on against the rush of air. When he waved Gordon felt himself very nearly swept away, but the djinn put up one huge hand and wrapped his fingers firmly round Gordon's wrist.

Soon he turned his head and shouted

over one shoulder, "Down there is my
part of the world."

Gordon could see a parched landscape
with hardly a dwelling in sight.

On they swept, now over the ocean, its huge waves shrunk to tiny blue crinkles. Below was a tiny green island, its edges marked white against the dark sea. By now the sun was above them, and burning their backs. On and on they flew.

"Your jumbo would have to refuel in Bangkok or somewhere," shouted the djinn, "but I have no need to stop. I shall go over the sea, it will be cooler than crossing central Australia."

There were more islands, and then they were flying along an endless coastline with thundering white surf. The sun was low in the sky on their right.

"That is Australia," said the djinn. "See, there is the Barrier Reef. And out there is the Pacific."

Some way out to sea far below were

paler turquoise patches, with now and
then a white breaking wave.

"We go down now," shouted the
djinn. "Keep swallowing." And Gordon
felt himself plunging down, down,

down until they were skimming the surface of the sea.

All at once Gordon saw the sharp fin of a cruising shark, and then another and another. Everywhere he looked he could see them, a whole mass of sharks.

He gave a gasp of fear.

The djinn heard him, gave a comforting squeeze to his wrist, and flew up higher. After a minute or so he turned towards the coast, gliding round in a huge circle, gently losing height and speed.

# Seven

In the distance, on a beach of yellow sand, Gordon could see a group of people in swimming costumes. They had a barbecue going, and some of them were sitting round it, some lying stretched out in the evening sun. As he watched, one of them left the group and walked down towards the sea.

There was a narrow jetty which stretched out beyond a line of netting, over deeper water. The lone figure stepped on to the jetty and walked towards the end. There was a small boat tied half-way along, but she didn't get into it, she went on walking.

"Hurry," shouted Gordon. "That must be her."

The djinn gave two quick beats with his wings, folded them to his sides and swooped towards her.

Too late. Miss Knight stood for a moment on the end, swung both arms above her head and dived in.

There was a warning shout from someone on the beach, and another from a life-guard. Gordon could see why. Speeding through the clear water from further out was the shadowy outline of a huge shark.

The djinn changed course and flew low over the shark. Gordon shouted, and flapped an arm, but it took no notice.

Miss Knight was floating on her back, quite unaware of any danger, while the shark was heading straight for her.

"Go back," shouted Gordon in the djinn's ear. The djinn banked sharply. Gordon slipped sideways, but clung on to the djinn's neck grimly. As soon as he'd righted himself he reached down

with one hand and ripped off one of his trainers.

As the djinn flew back over the shark, Gordon threw the trainer at it. It fell with a splash into the water. The shark

changed direction to investigate, and Gordon saw it rise right to the surface. There was a ripple and a smaller splash, and his trainer was gone.

By now there was loud shouting from the beach, and Gordon saw one of the life-guards leap into the boat and push it out from the jetty.

Miss Knight must have heard the shouts, because she began to swim towards the boat. But the shark was back again, following her. It was closing in.

"Quick," said Gordon to the djinn. "Again!"

Again the djinn swooped low over the shark, and Gordon hurled his other trainer at it. The shoe missed, and bobbed up and down in the water. The shark turned and swam after it, nosing it along.

Out of the corner of his eye Gordon saw Miss Knight swimming as fast as she could. She had reached the side of the boat. At the same split second the shark opened its huge jaws and closed them over his second trainer.

Then it turned its attention back to the
swimmer.

She was hauled into the boat,
snatching her feet to safety just in time.
The life-guard struck at the shark with
his paddle, and it thrashed its tail and
headed back out to sea.

"She will be safe now," said the djinn.
"O Master, you did well. We can leave
her."

He circled the beach once more,
gaining height with each powerful beat
of his wings.

Looking down, Gordon could see Miss
Knight being brought ashore in the boat,
and the excited knot of people who
gathered round. The life-guard had an
arm round her shoulders. Good old
Miss Knight, thought Gordon. He'd
have liked to give her a hug himself.

But the crowd on the sands was becoming smaller and smaller in the fading light as Gordon and the djinn rose higher and higher, until he could hardly make them out at all.

"Hold on tight!" shouted the djinn,

and they shot off westward towards the red sunset glow.

The return journey seemed to take longer, but at last they were back, flying above the grey woolly cloud which covered the English Channel, then descending through it and cruising gently down towards Selkirk Road.

There was a distant roll of thunder, a bright flash, and the djinn landed lightly in the middle of the carpet in Gordon's bedroom. He folded his wings and lifted Gordon down off his shoulders.

Everything was just as they had left it, completely normal, but when Gordon looked down he saw that his feet were blue with cold.

"Now you have had your three wishes," said the djinn. He bent down and blew warm breath over Gordon's feet.

"Thank you," said Gordon, sitting on the bed and tucking his feet under him. He could feel them glowing as the life came back to them. He gave a huge sigh of relief.

The clock on the bedside table said quarter past ten. How, Gordon wondered, was he going to explain his missing trainers?

"Just say you lost them," said the djinn. He straightened and stood looking down at him a little sadly. "Farewell, O Master. I must go now. Who knows, perhaps we may meet again." And he bowed low. Slowly he faded from sight. A few green shreds of smoke drifted towards the window and out into the street.

"Wait, wait!" cried Gordon, rushing to

the window, but there was nothing but a deep chuckle borne back on the wind.

Gordon ran downstairs to find his mother. She was sweeping the kitchen floor. "You're a bit late for any breakfast," she said. "I've cleared it all away now. Oh, and by the way, I tidied up all that junk that was in beside the football you bought. You didn't want it, did you? I gave that old lamp to the flower-seller woman who was at the car boot sale – she called just now."

"Oh," said Gordon. He grabbed a bowl of cereal and then went back up to his room. Beside his bed was the list he'd been going to make for Christmas presents. It was still blank, but for one word written unevenly in green ink: *Trainers*.

*Also in Young Puffin*

# The
# Village Dinosaur

**Phyllis Arkle**

**"What's going on?"**
**"Something exciting!"**
**"Where?"**
**"Down at the old quarry."**

It isn't every small boy who finds a living
dinosaur buried in a quarry, just as it
isn't every dinosaur that discovers Roman
remains and stops train smashes. Never
have so many exciting and improbable
things happened in one quiet village!

*Also in Young Puffin*

# The Air-Raid Shelter

**Jeremy Strong**

"Girls first. You go," said Adam.
"But you're the youngest," said
Rachel.
"You're the eldest," said Adam.
They stood there and looked at each
other with set faces.

When Adam and Rachel find an old air-raid shelter they are a little scared of how dark and smelly it seems. But it is the perfect place for a secret camp and with a little work it looks quite cosy...until it is discovered by the bullying Bradley boys.

# You Can't Say I'm

### Robert Swindells

**"Put that on," said the old man, "and you'll have the finest guy anybody ever saw."**

Gaz, Sophie, Jim and Pip are certain they'll win the Guy Fawkes competition with the mask that old Wurzel gives them. But magic in the mask gives them all a fright.

Then Gaz hides in a hollow tree, only to find that it's a strangely different world when he comes out.

Two original and highly enjoyable stories from a master storyteller.

# FANTASTIC MR FOX

### Roald Dahl

**Boggis, Bunce and Bean are just about the nastiest and meanest three farmers you could meet.**

And they hate Mr Fox. They are determined to get him. So they lie in wait outside his hole, each one crouching behind a tree with his gun loaded, ready to shoot, starve, or dig him out. But clever, handsome Mr Fox has other plans!

# THE Hodgeheg

**Dick King-Smith**

**Max is a hedgehog who becomes a
hodgeheg, who becomes a hero!**

The hedgehog family of Number 5A are a
happy bunch, but they dream of reaching
the Park.  Unfortunately, a very busy
road lies between them and their goal and
no one has found a way to cross it in
safety.  No one, that is, until the
determined young Max decides to solve
the problem once and for all...

*Also in Young Puffin*

# The Worst Child I Ever Had

### Anne Fine

**Snail parties, snail schools, snail feasts, a snail beauty shop, snail patterns and snail races – Susan Solly just loved snails!**

Sniffers, fussers, sneaky and bad-tempered children are all awful – but who's the worst child ever? Mrs Mackle is sure that it's Susan Solly. But what did she do that was so terrible? Find out in this entertaining and funny story by a prize-winning author.

*Also in Young Puffin*

# The Ghost *at* Codlin Castle
## and Other Stories

### Dick King-Smith

**Have you ever wondered what it's like to carry your head under your arm? Or tried to guess what garden gnomes get up to after dark?**

In this marvellously varied collection of stories, Dick King-Smith introduces some fascinating characters: a baby yeti, a bald hobgoblin and an extraordinary sausage-shaped alien among them.

Funny, mysterious, sinister, these gripping tales make ideal bedtime reading. With remarkable illustrations by Amanda Harvey, this is a book to stir the imagination.

# READ MORE IN PUFFIN

For children of all ages, Puffin represents quality and variety – the very best in publishing today around the world.

For complete information about books available from Puffin – and Penguin – and how to order them, contact us at the appropriate address below. Please note that for copyright reasons the selection of books varies from country to country.

**On the worldwide web**: www.puffin.co.uk

**In the United Kingdom**: Please write to *Dept. EP, Penguin Books Ltd, Bath Road, Harmondsworth, West Drayton, Middlesex UB7 ODA*

**In the United States**: Please write to *Consumer Sales, Penguin USA, P.O. Box 999, Dept. 17109, Bergenfield, New Jersey 07621-0120*. VISA and MasterCard holders call 1-800-253-6476 to order Penguin titles

**In Canada**: Please write to *Penguin Books Canada Ltd, 10 Alcorn Avenue, Suite 300, Toronto, Ontario M4V 3B2*

**In Australia**: Please write to *Penguin Books Australia Ltd, P.O. Box 257, Ringwood, Victoria 3134*

**In New Zealand**: Please write to *Penguin Books (NZ) Ltd, Private Bag 102902, North Shore Mail Centre, Auckland 10*

**In India**: Please write to *Penguin Books India Pvt Ltd, 706 Eros Apartments, 56 Nehru Place, New Delhi 110 019*

**In the Netherlands**: Please write to *Penguin Books Netherlands bv, Postbus 3507, NL-1001 AH Amsterdam*

**In Germany**: Please write to *Penguin Books Deutschland GmbH, Metzlerstrasse 26, 60594 Frankfurt am Main*

**In Spain**: Please write to *Penguin Books S. A., Bravo Murillo 19, 1° B, 28015 Madrid*

**In Italy**: Please write to *Penguin Italia s.r.l., Via Felice Casati 20, I 20124 Milano*

**In France**: Please write to *Penguin France S. A., 17 rue Lejeune, F-31000 Toulouse*

**In Japan**: Please write to *Penguin Books Japan, Ishikiribashi Building, 2-5-4, Suido, Bunkyo-ku, Tokyo 112*

**In South Africa**: Please write to *Longman Penguin Southern Africa (Pty) Ltd, Private Bag X08, Bertsham 2013*